AFRICAN TEA

ILLUSTRATIONS BY
LESLEY THOMSETT

WRITTEN BY CARTER SMITH

DEDICATED TO MY TWO BUSHBABIES
TIERNEY AND CHARLIE

AND TO BELLA
MAY SHE FOREVER SOAR THE SKIES

Once upon a time, in the golden grasslands of East Africa, there lived a fox named Timothy. Timothy was not just any fox. He was a bat-eared fox.

He lived in a little hole called a burrow in the middle of the savannah. His next-door neighbor was a porcupine named Madeline. Just a few tunnels away there was a warthog named Winston. Above ground there were many other animals that were friends and part of a community.

Late afternoon was the favorite time of day for Timothy and his friends. The sun was low on the horizon and its' golden rays touch the trees with magic. This was the time of day that the animals gathered around and had their afternoon tea under their favorite tree. They all looked forward to teatime. It gave everyone a chance to share the news of the day in the cool shade of the African umbrella tree.

Animals like Isaac the kingfisher and Penelope the giraffe relaxed at the end of the day and sipped their tea waiting for evening to come. Animals like Timothy and his neighbor Madeline were just starting their day, because their day-time was really night-time.

If everyone did not gather at teatime, many days would go by without seeing one another. And so it became a daily tradition.

One particular day, there was no news to share. Jeffry the dung beetle complained that the elephants had moved out of the savannah into a patch of forest. For the last couple of weeks there was no dung for him to roll.

Jackson the weaver bird chirped, "That is nothing to complain about! My house is falling apart! I have been trying to weave a new nest, but the grass is too short. It is too brittle because it is so dry. We have been without rain for so many months. I do hope it comes soon."

Isaac said, "Well, at least you are able to put food on the table. Imagine my distress without any fish! The rivers are completely dry."

Clyde the Wildebeest grumbled, "There is hardly any grass anywhere. The only grass I find is so short that I cannot reach it without hurting my back."

All of a sudden, there was a whooshing sound above everyone's heads. They looked up and saw Bella the Martial Eagle soar in and perch in the tree above them. They were very excited to see her. It was not everyday that Bella came for tea. She was always busy soaring in the sky to make sure that all was well down below. When Bella came for tea, it was because there was big news to report. They all gathered around, eager to hear what she had to say.

"Do you have any news Bella?" Jeffry said from his stump far beneath Bella.

"Don't be rude Jeffry. Would you like a cup of tea Bella?" asked Madeline politely.

"Yes, do have some tea, and then please tell us your news," Winston said kindly. He never forgot his manners.

"No thank you. No tea for me. I have indeed come with some news. We have something wonderful arriving any day now."

"What is it?" asked Penelope with excitement. "Who is coming?"

"Not who Penelope, but what. The rains are coming very soon," said Bella in her regal voice. "And once the rain comes, everything will grow and bloom and be beautiful once again."

"The river beds will flow and be full of fish!" shouted Isaac.

"Our troubles will be solved. The rainy season is the best time of year! The grass will grow in no time," Winston added.

Jeffry said, "What I look forward to the most when the rains come, is that the heat finally breaks. The heat gets simply unbearable way down here on the sun-baked ground."

Jackson noticed that Timothy looked unhappy. His head hung low and his big ears drooped.

"What is the matter Timothy? You are not your cheery self this afternoon? You haven't said a word."

"Well, I am glad that the rains are on the way but…," stammered Timothy, "but my house will flood! Don't you remember what the last rains did to my Uncle Chester's house? Madeline, Winston, you live underground as well! Aren't you the slightest bit concerned?"

"Oh goodness, you are right! I do remember that Timothy," Winston gasped. "Your uncle was homeless for weeks due to the flooding. We collected books and a kitchen chair a month later on the bank of the river."

Suddenly, the excitement was gone and all was quiet. The animals became deeply troubled about their friends who lived underground.

"Well, we will just have to put our heads together and come up with a plan," said Bella positively. "Between all of us we will think of a solution." Bella looked down at Madeline who was always upbeat and cheerful. Madeline put down the teapot and leaned against Jeffry's stump. Her eyes were heavy with worry. "Madeline," said Bella, "we will find a solution."

"Time is ticking away Bella. You said that the rains are coming any day. It could be the end of the week before we have an idea how to save our burrows."

"I have a fantastic idea," chirped Jackson from his nest. " I can weave a door for your burrows. If I ask the other weaver birds to help, we can finish in no time. Surely before the rains come!"

"Oh what a splendid idea!" said Madeline.

"Thank you Jackson," said Bella. "Good luck." And with that, Bella flew into the sky and disappeared into the clouds.

"Goodness. It is late," said Jeffry, as he stretched. The sun was beginning to set. "We should call it a day. Thank heavens the rains are coming soon."

"Good luck with the weaving Jackson. And thank you," said Timothy.

"My pleasure. Weaving is what I do best. Have a nice night," Jackson said, remembering that for Timothy, Winston and Madeline, their day was just beginning. "By tomorrow at teatime we will have finished most of our work."

They all said their goodbyes and went their separate ways.

The next morning, Jackson and the other weaver birds started bright and early. Some collected grass while others began to weave as fast as they could. By early afternoon their spirits sank. They found the task next to impossible. Every other blade of grass they wove broke because it was too brittle. The grass that they could weave was too short and the doors they made were far too small.

Jackson looked up and saw his friends begin to gather under the umbrella tree. Much to his surprise, it was teatime already.

They settled in their usual places. Madeline began pour the tea. "The clouds are beginning to roll in already. Isn't it marvelous?"

"How is the weaving," Clyde the Wildebeest asked.

They all looked at Jackson. " I am afraid that my good idea really was not a good idea at all. I should have known. The grass is too short to keep up our nests properly. I do not know why I thought that we could weave doors large enough to cover the entrances to your burrows."

Timothy looked up at the sky. Bella was right. The rains were coming very soon. He would surely be without a house.

"Not to worry," Isaac said reassuringly. "We just have to come up with another plan."

"Ah-ha!" shouted Winston. "I know just the trick! Elaine will be able to solve the problem!"

"Elaine the trapdoor spider," questioned Penelope.

"Yes. She lives in the ground and has a trapdoor that blends in with the earth. No one can see it except for her family. That is how she stays safe. But surely it keeps her dry as well. I will ask her to built trapdoors for our burrows."

With the news of another plan floating in the air, everyone perked up. This plan was bound to work. Timothy smiled at the idea of having a trapdoor for his house. What fun he thought.

The animals sipped their tea and enjoyed the shade of the umbrella tree. As the sun began to meet the horizon, they all said their goodbyes and went their separate ways.

The next day, Winston trotted off with his tail in the air to the dry riverbed, where the beautiful yellow fever trees were. He knew Elaine's house was somewhere on the bank of the river. He had known her for years, but he still didn't know exactly where her house was, thanks to her trapdoor.

"Elaine? Elaine? It's Winston. Elaine?"

Suddenly, next to his back left hoof, Elaine popped her head out of the earth. "How nice to see you Winston, but you look worried about something."

Winston told Elaine that the rains were coming any day now and about the worries they had about their burrows. He asked if she could help.

"I would love to help, but that would be a huge job for me and my family. It would take us weeks just to complete one door. By then, the rains will have come and gone. I am so sorry to disappoint you, but we will not be able to help."

"It was just an idea," sighed Winston. "We will come up with another one."

"Do tell me how it turns out. Good luck," Elaine said sweetly.

Winston trotted back to the umbrella tree just in time for tea. He looked up at the sky and saw many dark clouds. "Oh dear, we are running out of time," he said to himself.

He could tell they were all anxiously waiting for him to share his news. He adjusted his monocle and began. "I am very sorry, but the job I asked Elaine to do will take her weeks to complete."

Just then, they heard the air parting over their heads. It was Bella! She perched above them and said, "The clouds are heavy with rain. They are going to break any time now. Run along everyone and find a warm place to watch the long awaited rains begin."

"What are we going to do," cried Timothy.

Bella said wisely, "Those of you who live in burrows, you shouldn't worry. The best ideas are sometimes the most simple. The solution will come when you least expect it."

"Don't be frightened Timothy," Madeline said bravely. "Just climb into your burrow and light a fire in the fireplace. The leaks in the ceiling always take time to start."

"How nice it is that you have a fire to keep you warm. All I can do is sit down in the grass and feel the rain trickle down my neck. I get awfully cold," said Penelope.

"That's it! I have a solution," said Bella. "Giraffes like to sit down in the grass when it rains. Why don't you sit on top of Timothy's burrow? That will prevent the rain from coming in. Your friends can do the same with Madeline and Winston's houses. You can keep warm by the fire burning in their houses down below."

"What a magnificent idea, and so simple," Madeline exclaimed. "Penelope and all of the other giraffe stay warm while we stay dry. Clyde, you and your friends can do the same!"

They danced around with excitement. Then they realized that they were beginning to get wet. The rains had started! They quickly gulped down their tea and ran for cover.

Timothy dashed to his burrow and made a roaring fire. He felt safe knowing that Penelope was sitting just above him.

Penelope settled down on top of Timothy's house. She enjoyed the soft raindrops that ran down her neck and the smoke from the fire below that warmed her tummy.

Isaac rushed over to his favorite tree on the riverbank. It gave him a perfect view of the river that had already begun to rise.

The raindrops turned into a steady rainstorm, which continued all night. The animals were safe and warm.

The next morning was just beautiful. The sun peaked through the clouds and touched the rain soaked ground. The golden grasslands had a hint of green and wildflowers began to bloom.

The river started to flow and the fish returned. In just one day, the rains brought the grasslands to life.

The heavy clouds gathered again the next evening and the evening after that. The rains had finally arrived and the animals had a spring in their step once again.

Made in the USA
Columbia, SC
24 February 2018